The Litter Knight

Syd Hoff

McGRAW-HILL BOOK COMPANY
New York • Toronto • St. Louis • San Francisco

Library of Congress Catalog Card Number: 75-107291
ISBN 07-029188-8R 029189-6L
4567890 HDEC 754321

In days of old when knights were bold, there was one knight who was afraid of a fly. His name was Sir Dudley.

"Flies bring germs and germs cause disease," he told the other knights.

They laughed at him. "Who's afraid of germs? We're bigger than they are, anyway."

But Sir Dudley kept on watching for flies. He put screens on the palace windows.

While the other knights practiced fighting, Sir Dudley would worry about the litter on the field and the picnic lunches in the grandstands.

"All that trash," thought Sir Dudley, "with nobody to clean it up."

And while he worried, some knight would come along and knock him off his horse, yelling, "Pay attention to the tournament!"

But Sir Dudley didn't care about tournaments. He only cared about the apple cores, banana skins, and chicken bones that he saw around him.

"There must be something I can do about the situation," he said, and went riding off to see.

He used his lance to pick up the trash that littered the countryside.

He used his shield to cover up garbage cans.

He even stopped riding. Instead, his faithful horse helped carry loads of refuse far out of town.

The people appreciated that. There were hardly any sanitation rules in the Kingdom and all they wanted was a chance to breathe fresh air for a change. For while the King always remembered to collect the taxes. he usually forgot to collect the garbage.

But the King, who always had a stuffed nose and could hardly breathe anyway, flew into a rage when he heard of Sir Dudley's daily rounds.

"You call yourself a knight?" he screamed. "Then act like one! Go into the Dark Forest and slay a dragon!"

Sir Dudley hated the idea because he had nothing against dragons personally. Besides, he thought the garbage problem was much more urgent. Still, he wanted to be a good knight, and orders were orders.

So he rode forth into the Dark Forest.

"How can I carry out the King's orders?" he asked the dragons, in great distress. "You poor creatures can't help it if you breathe fire."

Now the dragons liked Sir Dudley. He had never tried to harm a scale of their heads and he always had a kind word for them.

"We'll go into hiding," they said, taking care not to breathe on him, "and the King will think you got rid of us."

Sir Dudley hurried back to the palace with the good news.

"Your Majesty," he reported, "the dragon problem is solved."

The king didn't believe it. The other knights didn't believe it. But when they went out into the Dark Forest and saw families having picnics, they believed it.

The King ordered a great feast to be held in the courtyard, in Sir Dudley's honor, and the best people came to the palace.

They ate great quantities of food and threw away the scraps without caring where they landed.

Then they all went home, still dropping litter, and everyone in the palace went to bed.

But Sir Dudley couldn't sleep. He was worried about all that waste and litter, and the flies it would attract.

He got out of bed and once more started collecting the garbage.

The King came chasing after him. "You're hopeless!" he screamed. "What's more, you're a disgrace to knighthood! I hereby banish you from the Kingdom!"

And so Sir Dudley rode forth again into the Dark Forest, this time to say goodbye to the dragons, and to tell them of the huge pile of litter he was leaving behind.

"Maybe we can help you dispose of it before you leave," said the dragons, and they lined up to follow Sir Dudley back to town.

At the sight of the dragons, everyone began to run —especially the King and the other knights. But the dragons headed straight for the garbage and breathed on it.

Soon all the garbage was burned to ashes. A light breeze blew the smoke away.

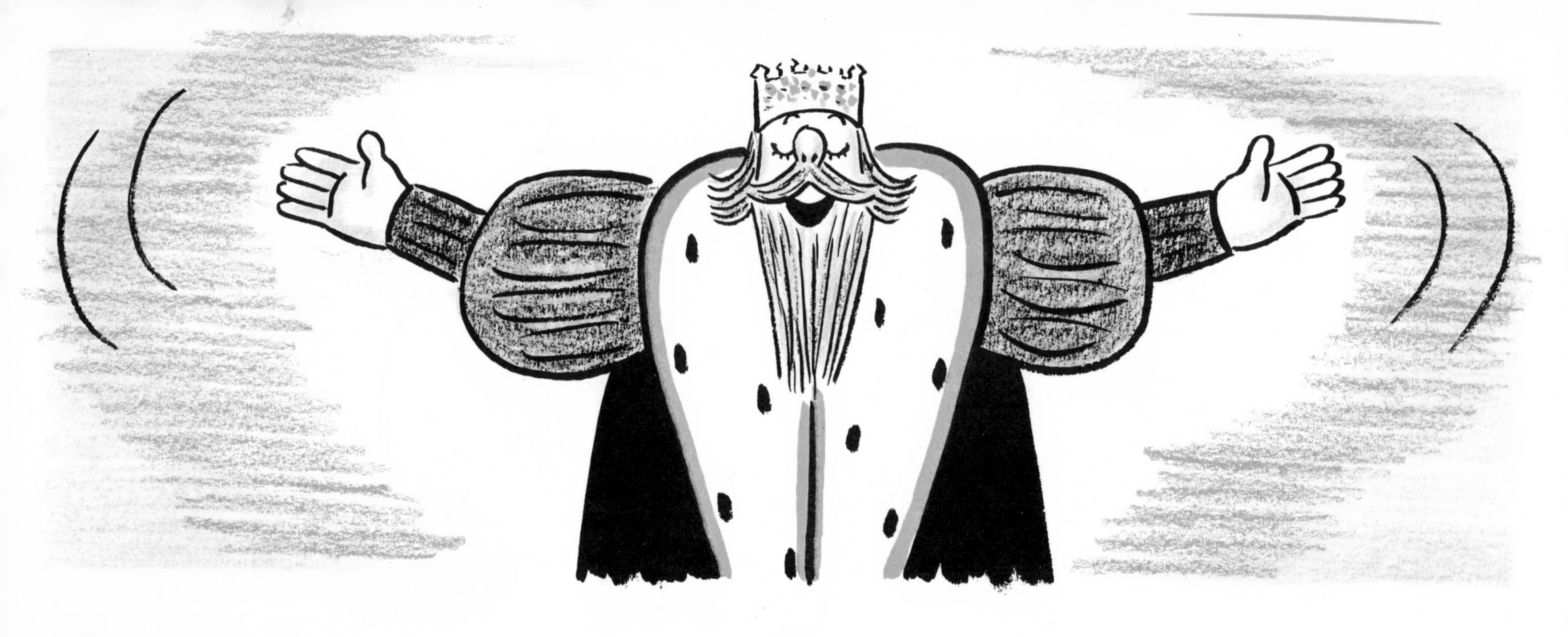

“Hooray for Sir Dudley! Hooray for the dragons!” shouted the King. The sudden rush of fresh air had opened his nose and he was able to breathe for the first time in years.

“Quick,” he cried. “Collect those ashes and bury them. Now that we have fresh air, we don’t want to lose it again.” And he ordered another feast.

“From now on, we’ll take care of our own litter, so the dragons can go back home to the Dark Forest,” said the King. And he wanted to thank Sir Dudley, but it was time to collect the garbage again.